To my nieces and nephews,
who always have a home in my heart
—BL

For Sky and Luna—my little galaxy
—ND

When the Stars Came Home

WRITTEN BY **BRITTANY LUBY**

PICTURES BY **NATASHA DONOVAN**

LB

Little, Brown and Company

New York Boston

"Home is under your hat," Mishomis always told Ojiig. But Mishomis never had to move his hat to the city like Ojiig did when his father got a government job.

In the city, Ojiig felt like a stranger in his own skin.

His family no longer fished from the river; they bought fish, already scaled, from the grocery store.

His family no longer picked blueberries; they bought those too—some as big as coins—frozen in a bag.

His neighbors said "hello," instead of "boozhoo." Mostly his neighbors said nothing at all. City folk paid more attention to park ducks than they did to him.

Worst of all, the sky no longer twinkled with starlight. Without the stars watching over him and listening to his secrets, Ojiig felt alone.

Ojiig learned to like softer fish and bigger blueberries. He greeted the ducks.

But Ojiig missed listening to Mishomis tell stories, he missed watching Kookum comb her long thick hair, and he missed seeing the stars.

He longed to trace the Milky Way with his fingers before falling asleep.

In the city, the streetlights were so bright that Ojiig had to squeeze his eyes tight as a fist to fall asleep.

One night, Ojiig felt sadness settle on his chest. “Mama!” he cried. “I want to go home.”

Mama took Ojiig into her arms, rocked him gently, and sang about the wonders of the night sky until he fell asleep.

When Ojiig woke, Mama was already in her going-out clothes. Papa too. "Ojiig," they said, "we will find a way to make the city feel like home. We are going to hunt for stars."

Ojiig got dressed lightning fast.
They walked the streets, scouring
local shops until they found
glow-in-the-dark stickers cut like stars.

At home, Mama and Ojiig stuck these stars to the walls of his bedroom. Papa put stars on the ceiling. Ojiig's room was filled with his favorite constellations.

But it was not the same. When star stickers fell, they floated to the floor. They did not blaze across the sky.

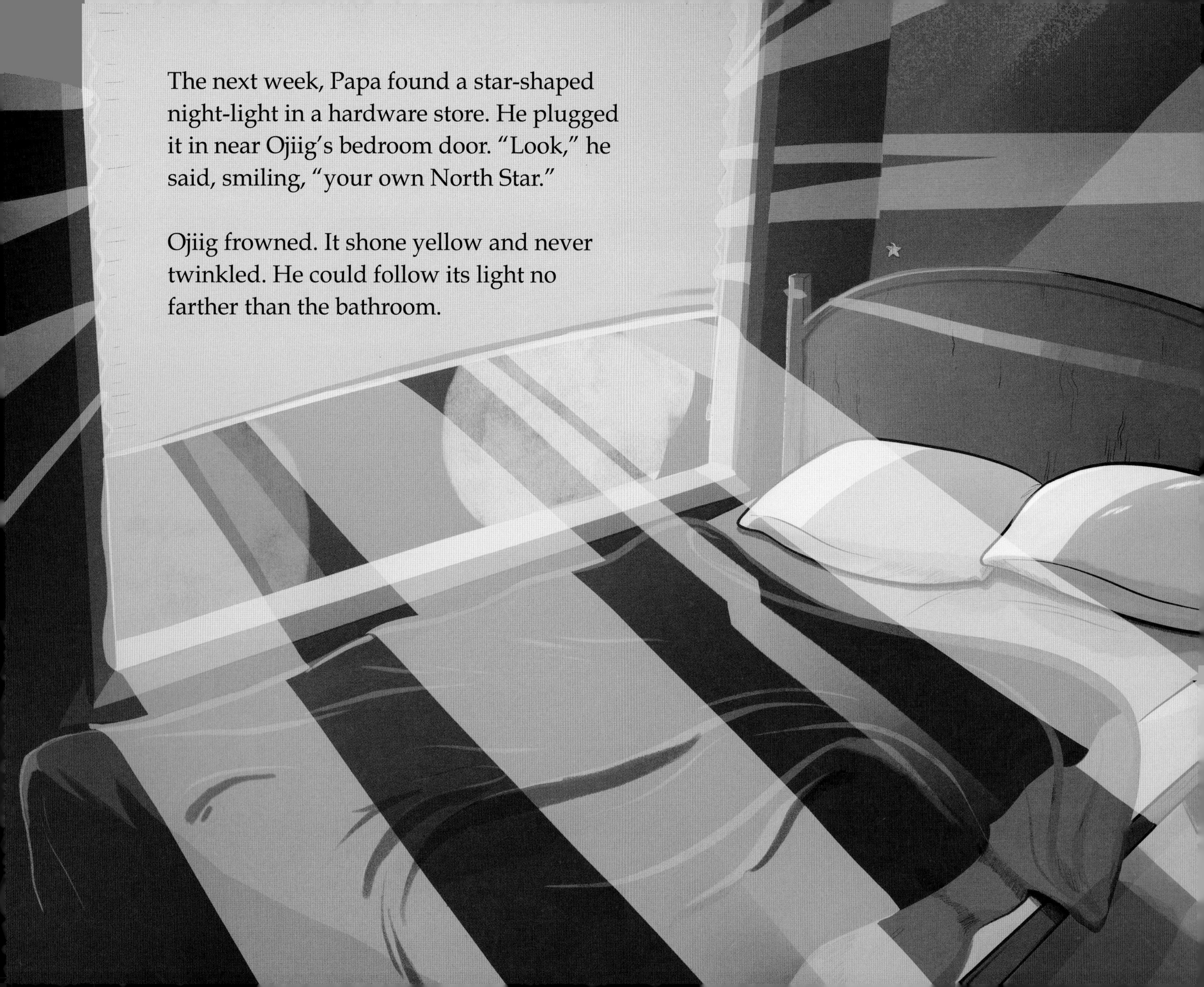

The next week, Papa found a star-shaped night-light in a hardware store. He plugged it in near Ojiig's bedroom door. "Look," he said, smiling, "your own North Star."

Ojiig frowned. It shone yellow and never twinkled. He could follow its light no farther than the bathroom.

Days passed. Ojiig didn't know how to wish anymore.

He unplugged his night-light.

One morning, he heard Mama call to him. "Ojiig, can you help me?" she asked.

Ojiig followed Mama's voice to the living room. There were many fabric triangles on the floor.

"I'm making a quilt," Mama explained.
"Pass me a white triangle."

As Mama sewed the white triangle onto a black square, she told Ojiig about his great-grandmother whose hair was as white as a seagull feather. She'd sung like a sparrow while preparing bannock over the fire. "Singing sweetens the bread," she'd said.

When Mama finished, she asked
Ojiig to pass her a yellow triangle.

As Mama stitched it into place, she told Ojiig about his great-grandfather whose skin once yellowed from fever. He'd gotten sick after rescuing a sled pup who had wandered too close to the beaver pond. After that, the pair was inseparable and, in time, became the fastest sled team around.

Ojiig liked to help Mama as she sewed. Each triangle held a story.

When Ojiig passed Mama a red triangle, he learned that another great-grandmother had hidden in a sack of potatoes whenever the government agent came looking for Indigenous children to take away to Boarding School. She had taught her children that red potatoes combined with quick wit were more valuable than gold.

And as Mama stitched an orange triangle into place, she smiled. Ojiig learned that another great-grandfather, crowned with the orange locks of his ancestors, came from across the sea. Some kids had pulled his hair. Others had teased. "But your great-grandfather said his hair was a blessing. He met your great-grandmother because he stood out in a crowd."

One day, Mama called Papa and Ojiig into the room. The quilt was finished!

Ojiig held his breath with excitement. He had only seen triangles and squares. Mama had been keeping the full pattern a surprise.

Mama shook out the quilt to reveal a giant star.

When Mama wrapped the quilt around Ojiig's shoulders, he beamed more brightly than the brightest star in the sky. He thought about all the stories his mama had stitched into the quilt. He thought about how all his ancestors' stories lived inside him. And he wondered what kinds of stories future generations might tell about him.

His thoughts were interrupted by knocking.

He followed Mama and Papa to the door. When it swung open, Mishomis and Kookum stepped in. Ojiig threw his arms around his grandparents.

Mishomis teasingly took off his hat, putting it on Ojiig's head.

"Did you find home under your hat?" Mishomis joked.

Ojiig laughed. He knew now that home had nothing to do with hats.

Home is where you learn who came before you.
Home is where you discover who you are.
Home is where you imagine who you might become.

Author's Note

When I left home for university, a journey that would take me past Lake Superior to the shore of Lake Ontario, a dear friend gifted me with a star blanket. Wrapping myself in that blanket when I felt alone was a comfort that allowed me to feel connected to the place and people I came from.

There is a long history of Indigenous children being pushed from their homes. Some of these children were forced into Boarding Schools (also known as Residential Schools) by government representatives called "Indian agents." Some Indigenous youth continue to face pressure to leave home in search of education because colonial governments, like the Dominion of Canada, underfunded schools on reserves for many years. Others, like Ojiig, accompany their guardians if they move to a nearby city in search of work.

Some urban Indigenous schools exist, but children removed from their cultural educators are often taught settler ways at school. Generations ago, when Dakota girls were taught to quilt in the settler tradition, some created star blankets. The messages conveyed by this new style of quilting took on cultural significance over time. Because people can look to the stars for direction, star blankets are sometimes given as gifts at life events, such as births and marriages.

The Dakota shared this indigenized quilting tradition with Anishinaabeg. Today, star blankets are woven into the cultural fabric of both Nations. In this story, Ojiig's mother—an Anishinaabe woman—uses the star blanket to help Ojiig feel at home in the city. Like the star blanket I cherished when I left home, it serves as a reminder that families are held together, no matter the distance, with love.

I am grateful to Kim A., Chelsea B., Dawn O., and Cara W. for inspiring me to research the history of star blankets, and to Mary Ann C. for her feedback on the pronunciation guide. I also say "miigwech" to Leah Ann O. for the gift that became this story.